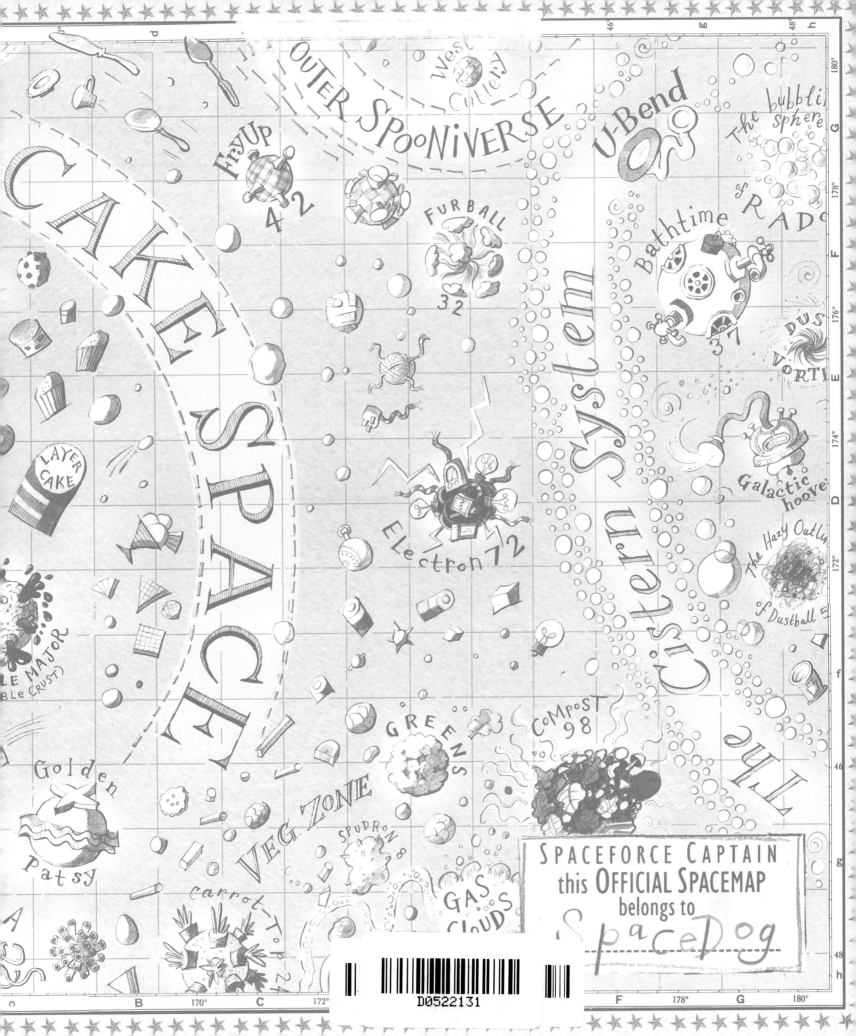

It's the year **3043** and, for as long as anyone can remember, on **HOME PLANET**

SPACE DOGS, **ASTRO**

have been **SWORN**

. . . in the vast deeps of space a small ship is zooming.

At last,
Space Dog
is about
to go

HOME

It has been a long mission sorting out planetary problems in the Dairy Quadrant.

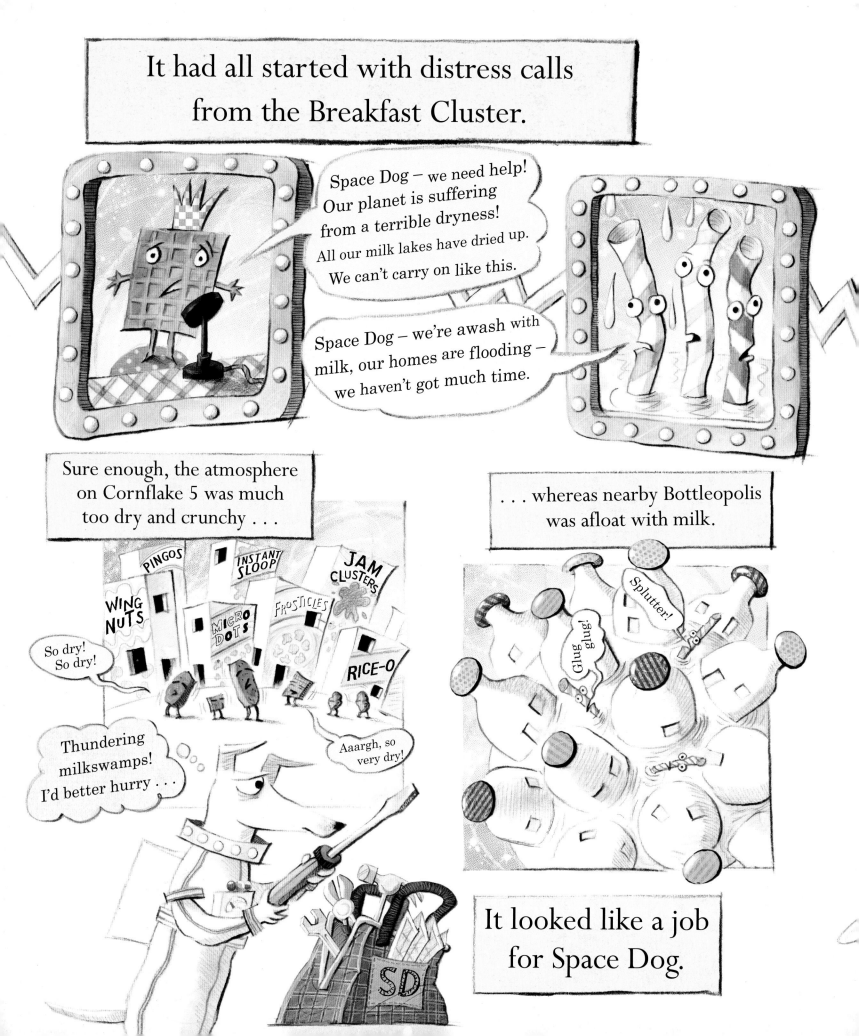

Things carried on . . .

with the evacuation of a Colossal Stink from Bath Time 37,

making contact with a Spaghetti Entity in the Pastaroid Belt, and rescuing the people of Niblet 12 from an escaped pet that had gone on the rampage.

Then there was just time to judge a hat competition . . .

. . . before Space Dog returned to his ship, the SS *Kennel*.

Time to go home.

At least there are plenty of supplies
in Space Dog's cupboard.

On board his ship
Space Dog has
his usual dinner,

* Sigh *

and then he plays
Dogopoly
on his own . . .

before he sleeps in his bunk
and dreams of his Home Planet,
shining like a beautiful marble
in space.

HOME PLANET

Meanwhile

somewhere not so far away in
the Dairy Quadrant, Astrocat is also
zooming in his saucer.

Mmmm, destination cream!

Suddenly Space Dog is woken by a distress call
coming through on his Laser Display Screen.

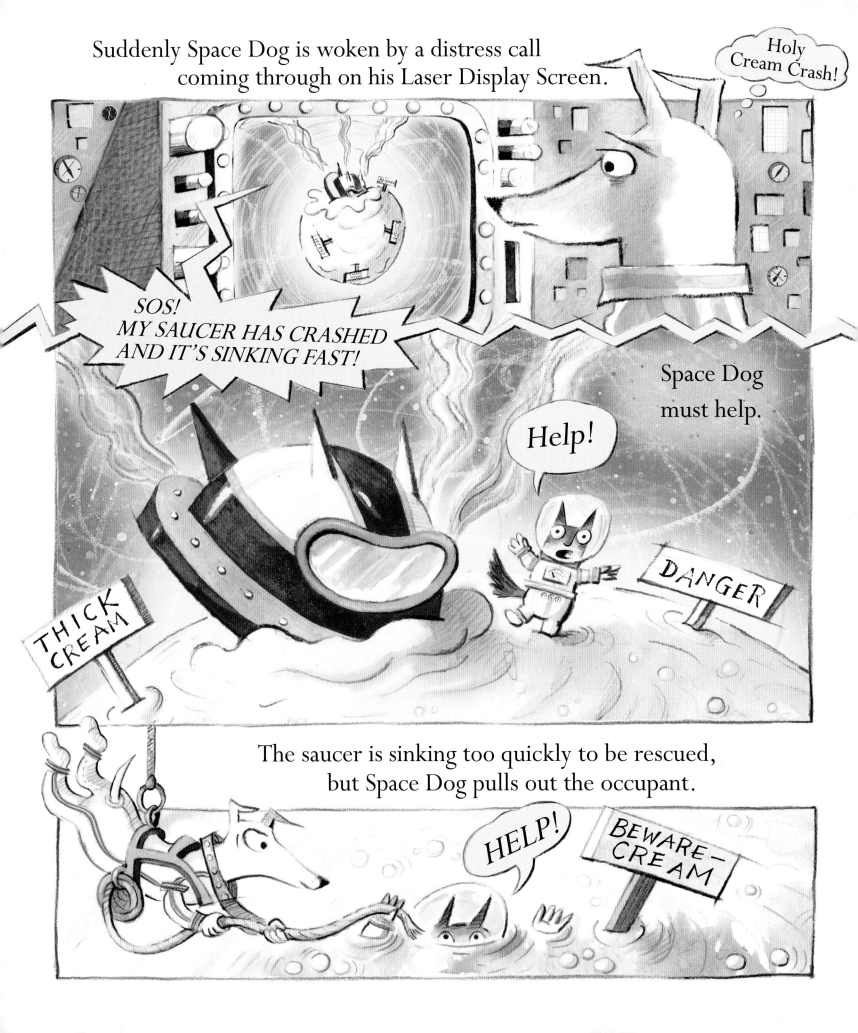

The saucer is sinking too quickly to be rescued,
but Space Dog pulls out the occupant.

AN ASTROCAT!

"But Astrocats and Space Dogs are Sworn Enemies!" gulps Astrocat.

"But there's no time for that now!" says Space Dog.

Space Dog drags Astrocat out of the thick cream and takes him aboard his own ship.

Your saucer is lost — you'd better hitch a ride in the SS *Kennel*.

GLUG

DANGER

What in CakeSpace am I going to do with an **Astrocat** on board?

When Astrocat has dried off . . .

I think you'll find, Space Dog, that your bone has landed on my kennel.

Well, I'll be jiggered! Not a bad move there, Astrocat. I'll have to up my game, playing you!

it turns out he is surprisingly good at playing Dogopoly,

Back on the ship, Space Dog is finally setting the controls for

HOME

The UNKNOWN

when —

HOME SWEET HOME

HELP!

No Pla...

WHIFF WHIFF

SOUVENIR OF EARTH

A distress call on the Laser Display Screen! Coming from this distinctly cheesy planet. They simply **have** to help.

And look —
a Moustronaut —
tied to a skewer over
a chasm of bubbling fondue.

"Be off with you,
Cheese Ants!"
cries Space Dog.

The ants scuttle away.

"Grab my tail, Space Dog," says Astrocat,
balancing precariously and untangling the rope.

"BUT MOUSTRONAUTS AND ASTROCATS ARE SWORN ENEMIES!"
gasps the Moustronaut.
"But there's no time
for that now!"
Astrocat replies.

"MY SATCHEL!
MY SATCHEL!"
screams the
Moustronaut.

Astrocat grabs the satchel,
and, getting ready to run,
they turn round
to see . . .

the Queen of the Cheese Ants –
and she doesn't look happy.

NING

NING

NING

NING

fromage

"She seems to be interested in what's in your satchel, Moustronaut," says Space Dog.

Her mandibles are dribbling and there's a hungry look in her compound eyes.

But then the Moustronaut has an idea.

She offers the Queen the cheese samples from her satchel —

rare samples from the farthest reaches of space — and bows respectfully.

Fromage

The Queen lowers her feelers.

The cheese samples must have been what she wanted. She must be a cheese collector too!

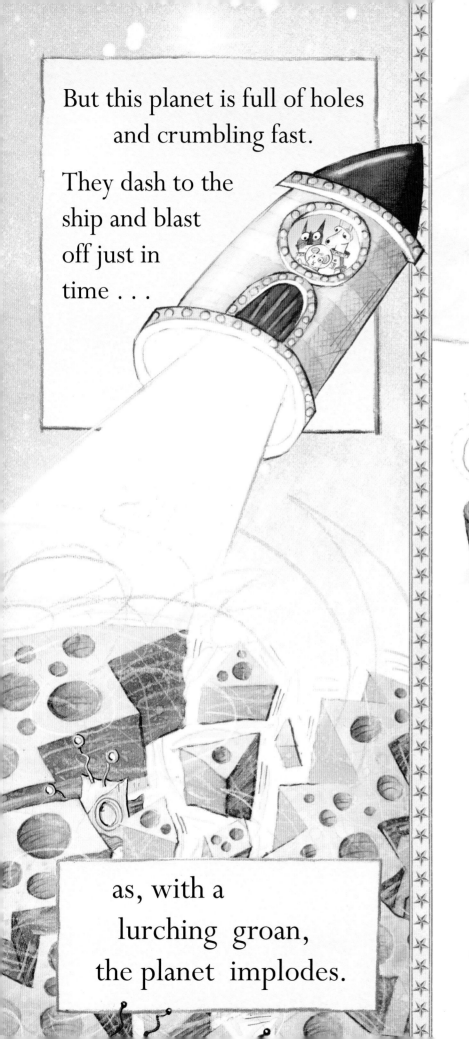

But this planet is full of holes and crumbling fast.

They dash to the ship and blast off just in time . . .

as, with a lurching groan, the planet implodes.

On board Space Dog's ship, they scrape the cheesy goo off the Moustronaut, and Astrocat runs her a nice bath.

But the Moustronaut has not only lost her precious cheese samples, but her Module too.

Very Important Cheese

"Cheer up, Moustronaut," says Astrocat.
"We need a quick-thinking mouse in our team.

Someone
with nimble fingers

and amazing
powers of sniff."

"Yes," says
Space Dog.

"Someone who is brave in
the face of giant insects,

and a third player
for Dogopoly.

Now we can go Home."

BACK TO...

HOME PLANET — WHERE SPACE DOGS, ASTROCATS AND MOUSTRONAUTS CAN BE

ENEMIES   FOR EVER

Everyone is quiet for a moment.   And then . . .

"BUT THERE'S NO TIME FOR THAT NOW!"

cries the Moustronaut. "THERE'S A WHOLE UNIVERSE OUT THERE -

ONE WHERE SPACE DOGS, ASTROCATS AND MOUSTRONAUTS CAN BE SWORN FRIENDS."

HOME

Near to the
Home button
on his control panel
is another one that
Space Dog hasn't
noticed before.

THE
UNKNOWN
ZONE

"Shall we?"
"OF COURSE!"
"Why not!"

And they set
controls for
THE
UNKNOWN
ZONE.

In the vast deeps of space
a small ship is zooming.
Adventures could be
on the horizon,
or even just round
the corner.

But for now,
Space Dog, Astrocat and
the Moustronaut are playing
Dogopoly before dinner.

Nobody is *completely* sure
about the exact rules for Dogopoly . . .

. . . but it doesn't seem to matter.

Yoo-hoo!

Special thanks
to the cosmic
inspiration
of Ness.

SPACE DOG
A JONATHAN CAPE BOOK 978 0 857 55090 3
Published in Great Britain by Jonathan Cape,
an imprint of Random House Children's Publishers UK
A Penguin Random House Company

Penguin
Random House
UK
This edition published 2015

1 3 5 7 9 10 8 6 4 2

Copyright © Mini Grey, 2015

RANDOM HOUSE CHILDREN'S PUBLISHERS UK
61–63 Uxbridge Road, London W5 5SA
www.randomhousechildrens.co.uk
www.randomhouse.co.uk

Addresses for companies within The Random House Group Limited can be found at: www.randomhouse.co.uk/offices.htm
THE RANDOM HOUSE GROUP Limited Reg. No. 954009
A CIP catalogue record for this book is available from the British Library.

Printed and bound in China.

For
Nancy
and
Herbie

A GUIDE TO RARE LIFE FORMS OF THE OUTER SPOONIVERSE

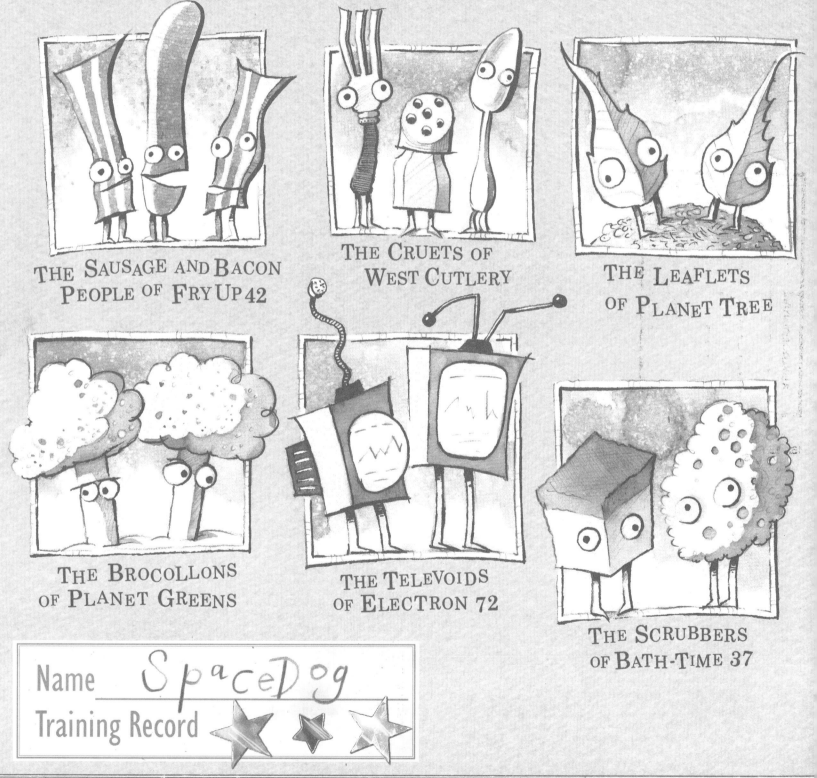

THE SAUSAGE AND BACON
PEOPLE OF FRY UP 42

THE CRUETS OF
WEST CUTLERY

THE LEAFLETS
OF PLANET TREE

THE BROCOLLONS
OF PLANET GREENS

THE TELEVOIDS
OF ELECTRON 72

THE SCRUBBERS
OF BATH-TIME 37

Name _Space Dog_

Training Record